This book belongs to

....

Copyright © 2019

make believe ideas ltd

The Wilderness, Berkhamsted, Hertfordshire, HP4 2AZ, UK.

www.makebelieveideas.com

5-MINUTE MAGICAL STORIES

make believe ideas

CONTENTS

We are the grOOvicOrns!

ROSIE GREENING ★ STUART LYNCH

Everyone **loves** unicorns. They always make a fuss.

But you know who **should** be famous?

I ♥ unicorns!

The grOOviCOrns!

That's us! ♥

The unicorns make **rainbows**

that **curve** from side to side.

but make
**amazing
slides!**

Unicorns sign hoofprints,

My Unicorn Scrapbook

To Rabbit,

Love Glitter

and they grant your **wishes**, too.

HAPPY BIRTHDAY

We don't have **magic powers,**

14

but we still make **dreams** come true!

15

Buckinghorn Palace

The unicorns build **palaces**

with sweet, **marshmallow walls.**

No adoring fans allowed

EEW, unicorn palaces are **GROSS!**

We have **multicoloured** tents

All Welcome

18

The unicorns **bring SUNSHINE** everywhere they go.

21

The sun is **super boring.** You know what's better?

SNOW!

The unicorns are bigheads — they **SHOW OFF** all day long.

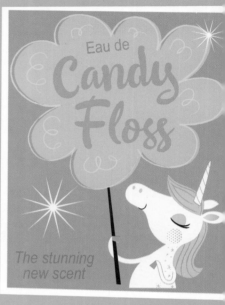

They **never** want to play with us, and —

 HEY!

Mane-gain!
Grow luscious locks in minutes

You've got it wrong.

 They're not THAT bad...

and this is how you **Sliiiiiiiiiiide.**

Nice rainbow, Ronald!

EVERYthing
is much more fun
if we **PLAY** side by side!

Everyone is different, but *special* in their way.

So let's **learn** from one another
and have more *fun* every day!

Just NARWHAL

Lara Ede • Rosie Greening

Narwhal was a whale who thought she had **no skills** at all.

She couldn't **cook**...

or knit...

or sing...

or even
catch a ball!

33

Meanwhile, all her **mermaid** friends
were skilful as can be.
If they tried out something **new**,
they did it **perfectly**.

"**Wow!**" thought Narwhal every day.
"There's nothing they can't do.
But I'm **just Narwhal**,
and I wish that I had **talent** too."

One morning, Star and Coral
cried to **Narwhal** in distress:

"Our **art contest** has started,
but everything's a **mess!**"

great
reef
painting
contest

JUDGING TODAY

"We need a **judge**," said Coral,
"and our time is nearly up.
Can **you** judge our paintings
and decide who wins this **cup?**"

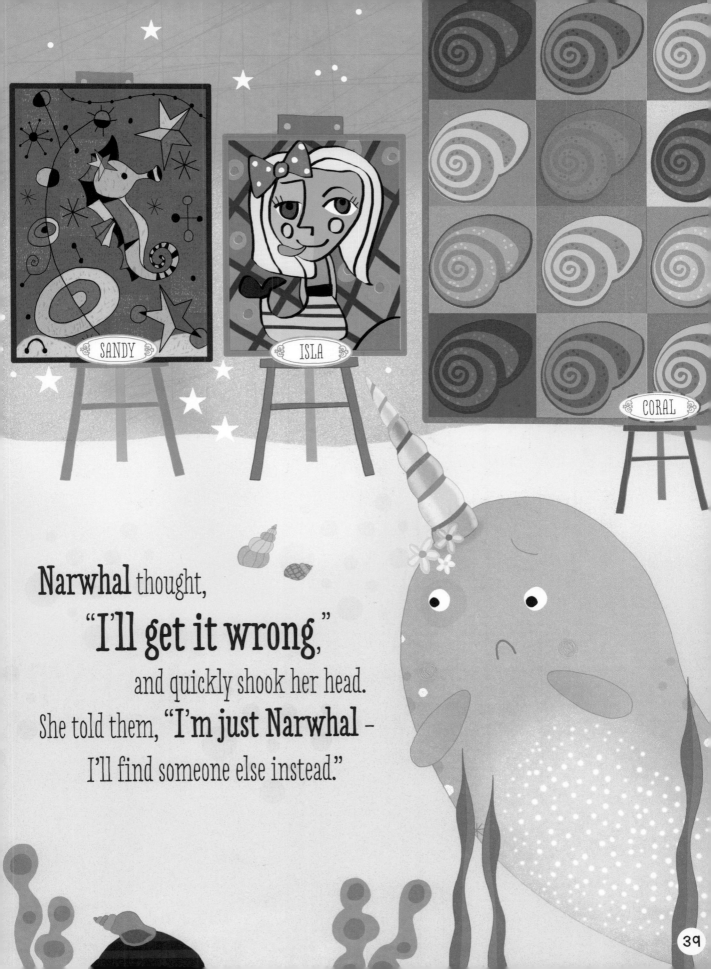

SANDY

ISLA

CORAL

Narwhal thought,
"I'll get it wrong,"
and quickly shook her head.
She told them, "I'm just Narwhal –
I'll find someone else instead."

She asked **Cackle the Clownfish**
to decide which art should win.

ISLA

"The prize goes to the
FUNNIEST!"
said Cackle with a grin.

Narwhal thought,
"That's not enough to win the special prize.
But I'm **just Narwhal**, so I'll check
with someone **big** and **wise**."

She found a **big blue whale** and asked,
"Which painting is the **best?**"

"The
BIGGEST!"
shouted Jumbo.
"**Forget** about the rest!"

"I'm not sure size is **everything**," said Narwhal quietly.
"But since I am **just Narwhal**,
I should check **Shelly** agrees."

Shelly scuttled round the art, but judged them **selfishly**.
The shellfish said, "The **winner** is the one that features . . .

ME!"

MARINA

Narwhal looked around and thought,
"These choices **don't** seem fair.

ISLA

CORAL

MARINA

They **can't** judge on **one thing** alone:
there's **much** more to compare."

Narwhal swam to join her friends.
"I've let you down!" she cried.

"You need a **fair** and **honest** judge,
who sees how **hard** you tried."

The mermaids said, "If that's the case,
then **YOU** should judge our art!
To us, you're not '**just Narwhal**',
and we'd **love** you to take part."

49

Narwhal gave a
nervous smile and said,
"Ok, I'll try!"

And she wrote a list of **qualities**
to judge the paintings by.

Narwhal swam around the art,
and **studied** each with care.
She looked at **every** brush stroke
to make sure that she was **fair**.

• Colours
• Theme
• Brushstroke
• Technique
• Effort
• Beauty

ISLA

SANDY

At last she said, "Each piece of art
is **special** in its way.
But **ONE** ticked every box for me . . .

Star wins first prize today!"

Star held up the shining cup
for **everyone** to see.
Then Coral rushed to Narwhal
and she **hugged** her gratefully.

She said, "You are the **finest** judge
we could have ever found.
You're **fair** and **open-minded**...

...the most
JUST narwhal around!"

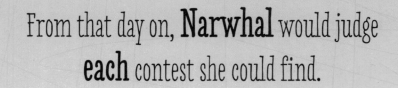

From that day on, **Narwhal** would judge **each** contest she could find.

And though she couldn't dance or sing, at last, she didn't **mind**.

She thought,

"My **skills** are hidden –
they're not **obvious** to see.
But just like all the **paintings,**

there is so much more to me!"

Mermaid Mia

and the Royal Visit

Lara Ede · Rosie Greening

Mermaid Mia loved to write *new* **stories** every day.

Ideas

She ran the **paper** at her school with **Emily** and **Fay**.

Emily took the **photographs**...

Say cheese!

and Fay did the **reviews.**

The Mermail

But **Mia** was the one in charge of each day's **front-page** news.

Mia's news was **popular**,
and **always** told with style.

Wow!
What a story!

Haha!

The Mermail

The Mermail

The Mermail

The Mermail

She was funny, frank and honest,
and her **words** made people smile.

One morning, **Mia** longed to find a juicy piece of **news.**

She got her **pad** and went in **search** of **something** she could use.

64

Her first lead was a story
on the **snails** in the canteen.

But the **news** was **SO** s-l-o-w-m-o-v-i-n-g, Mia **really** wasn't keen.

Then she heard a **rumour** of a **whale** stuck in the **gym**.

"Now **that's** a story," **Mia** thought. "I'll write my news on him!"

1, 2, 3, push!

STARFISH ACA[DEMY]

But just as **Mia** reached the **whale**, he managed to get **out**.

"My front page will be bare!"
she cried.
"What can I write about?"

Suddenly, a sneaky thought **popped** into **Mia's** head.

"The **real** news isn't good enough –
I'll **make it up** instead!"

She **swam** back to the newsroom
and began to type at speed.

"This **news** will make a **splash**," she thought.
"They're **sure** to want a read!"

Queen Marina is one
of the most popular
royals under the sea.
Whether it's recycling
in the coral beds or
opening libraries,
the queen always
has a new project
on the go.
Just last month, it
was Queen Marina's
birthday. It was a
magical day, with
tasty treats, a
fintastic band
and comedy from
the clownfish.

The biggest gift Queen Marina received was
a beautiful carriage, though it has yet to be
used out in public. We believe she is saving it
for a special occasion...

The Mermail

As soon as it was printed,
Mia's words began to **spread,**

and the school **buzzed** with **excitement**
at the **front-page** news that said . . .

The Mermail

Queen Marina

The Royal Palace

A ROYAL VISIT!

Written by Mermaid Mia

Her Highness, Queen Marina will be visiting our school. She's heard of the academy and wants to meet us all!

It was all the **mermaids** talked about: the **best** news of the year!

In class, they'd whisper **happily**:

"The **Queen** is coming HERE!"

I can't wait!

I bet we'll have a ball.

But soon the **news** got out of hand, which made poor **Mia** fret.
And as the day drew closer, she kept **hoping** they'd **forget**.

With one week left, she told her friends:

"I've made a **big mistake.**

The **queen's** not **really** visiting –

the news I wrote was **fake!**"

"You **should** have told the **truth**," said Fay.
"But now we need a **plan**.
We'll tell the queen what happened
and then **fix** this if we can."

So **Mia** sent a **letter**
to the queen's **royal** address.

Queen Marina
The Royal Palace
Under the Sea

Collections:
Mon-Fri
7am

Please do not
put shells in
the postbox.

She asked the queen to **help** them out,
and **hoped** that she'd say **yes**.

Soon, the **royal whale mail** delivered them a note.

You've got mail!

Mermaid Mia
Starfish Academy
Under the Sea

It was signed "Love, **Queen Marina**,"
and this is what she wrote . . .

Dear Mia,

You're very brave for owning up —
it's not easy to do.
And thank you for inviting me,
I'd love to visit you!

Love,
Queen Marina

At last, the **special** day arrived:
the **mermaids** couldn't wait.

They lined the school with **pretty flags**,
and a **sign** that said, "YOU'RE GREAT!"

The **queen** swam up to meet them all, and Mia **beamed** with **pride**.

The day was so **amazing**, Mia knew what she **should** do.

Miss Isabella meets Queen Marina

The queen's new fitness plan is a slam dunk!

Star student shows off her winning formula

The queen receives a warm welcome

She put the story in the **news**, and every word was **true**.

Everyone had a sea-riously good time!

Snail surprise

A ROYAL SUCCESS!

Written by Mermaid Mia

We had a great time yesterday
with Queen Marina here.
And as she left, she told us all:
"I'll come again next year!"

After that, **Mia** was **truthful**,
even when the news was **slow**.

She'd **learnt** that being **honest**
was the **only** way to **go!**

Alice
the
Amber
Fairy
and the Showstopper Spectacular

Sarah Creese * Lara Ede

In **Sparkle Town,** for all to see,
there stood a dazzling store
full of **amber instruments,**
and with a **singing** door!

High Street

Chief Creator of things to play,
for every kind of **sound**,

was **Alice** the **Amber Fairy** —
the best inventor around!

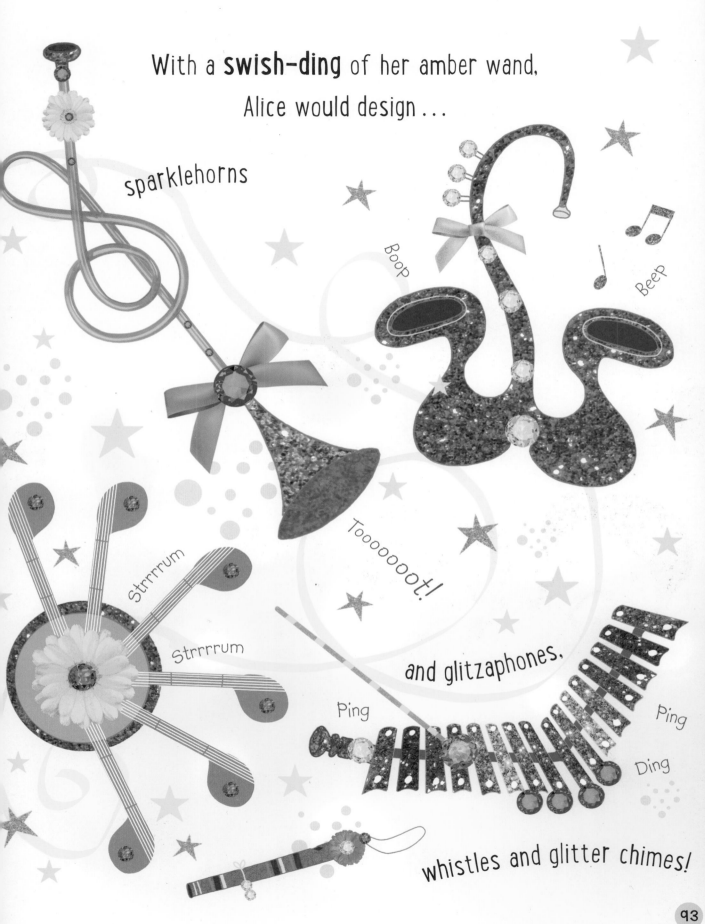

With a **swish-ding** of her amber wand,
Alice would design...

sparklehorns

Boop

Beep

Strrrrum

Strrrrum

Toooooot!

and glitzaphones,

Ping

Ping

Ding

whistles and glitter chimes!

Each **four years** in Fairy Land,
a contest came to town
to choose a **fairy winner** for
the SHOWSTOPPER SPECTACULAR crown.

High Street

Dear Fairies,

We proudly present the

SHOWSTOPPER SPECTACULAR

Fairy Land's greatest musical contest!

All tuneful entries will be welcomed.
but only **one** will be worthy of winning the **crown**.

Yours sincerely

Juno Jewel

SHOWSTOPPER SPECTACULAR Head Judge

It's Showstopper time!

Annie Amber

Alfie Amber

Alyssa Amber

The **Amber family** fairies
had won year in, year out.
So Alice's friends thought she would win —
of this, they had no doubt.

Ava Amber

Albert Amber

Agnes Amber

Amber Family Trophies

You're sure
to win.

96

The **problem** was, poor Alice

(please promise you won't tell)

could not play **ANY** instrument

particularly well.

Too scared to tell her friends the truth

or let her family down,

Alice cried, "What can I do?

How will I win the crown?"

First she tried
the **glitzaphone**
but her fingers
were too slow,

Then she tried
the **sparklehorn**
but her "toots"
came out too low.

The **glitter chimes** all clashed together,

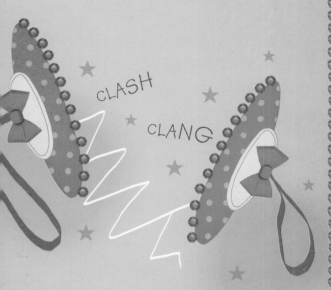

CLASH

CLANG

the bells went

ding,

dong,

wrong!

Rinnnnnng

Her **drumming** sounded too offbeat and the cymbals rang too long!

So Alice **worked** all through the night,
inventing **more** and **more**
until she created something
unlike anything seen before...

High Street

She took a breath, then blew inside
and **without touching a key,**

the instrument played **ON ITS OWN,**

and was **TUNEFUL** as can be!

Alice practised "**playing**"
to make her act look true
until she was finally ready for
her **Showstopper debut**.

The contest day arrived at last;
the fairies chatted together.

Said Esme,
"I've learnt mine by heart."

Said Susie,
"Mine sounds better!"

As Alice watched each one perform
and play their part with pride,
she felt **guilty** about tricking them
and knew she could not lie.

Alice was called to start her piece,
and the crowd let out a cheer
(for Alice's music was the act
they most wanted to hear).

"Umm...before I start," said Alice,
"there's something I **must** say.
I'm not a good musician;
in truth, I **cannot play**.

I **created** this machine
to cover up who I am.
This instrument plays on its own;
I'm really just a **sham**."

The fairies **gasped** together. They hadn't expected that!
As Alice began to tremble, Esme appeared from the back.

Well, that was a surprise.

Oh, my!

She smiled and hugged poor Alice.
"Don't feel blue," she said.
"You may not be a **Showstopper**,
but you're our **inventor** instead."

Alice did not play her piece,
and the **Showstopper** was won
by the most deserving fairy,
chosen by everyone.

Hurrah!

110

Go on, Alice!

WINNER

At the **afterparty** later,
the fairies all agreed:
there was one thing that the party
did really, truly need.

They cried to Alice all at once,
"We want to hear you play!"
So Alice grinned and took a breath
and without further delay . . .

it went...

Toot-Toot, la-de-da,

BEEP and fiddle dee dee;

a-ring-a-ling, BING-BANG

oompah-ooh and WHEEEEEEE!

Though the special instrument
was **famous** near and far,

Alice learnt that **best** of all
is being **who you are!**

Meet the Unicorns

Shannon Hays • Alexandra Robinson

Meet the Unicorns

Come and meet the unicorns.
They're friendly, sweet and fun.
You'll find them splashing in a stream
or playing in the sun.

Wish Upon a Horn

The unicorns have spiral horns
that give them magic powers
to grant your wishes every day
and fill green fields with flowers.

Magical Manes

They love to plait and decorate
their soft and glossy manes
with diamonds, gems and pretty bows
or strings of daisy chains.

The Royal Unicorns

These unicorns live far away
in castles made of jewels.
They all have chocolate fountains
and big, sparkly swimming pools.

The Rainbow Unicorns

These unicorns have rainbow wings
and gallop through the sky.
They paint pink clouds and rainbows
as they swoop and soar and fly.

The Flower Unicorns

In spring, the flower unicorns
are found near cherry trees.
They race across pink meadows
with the butterflies and bees.

The Snowflake Unicorns

These unicorns wear cosy coats
in cold and frosty weather.
They love to skate on frozen lakes
and glide around together.

The Midnight Unicorns

When midnight strikes, these unicorns
can brighten up the night.
They use their horns to make the stars
and fill the sky with light.

Now you've met the unicorns,
and made some special friends.
Come back to see them any time:
true friendship never ends!

Meghan Sparkle
and the ROYAL BABY

Lara Ede • Rosie Greening

Once, in **Coral Kingdom**, an announcement came to say
that a brand-new **royal baby** had been born that very day!

The King &
Queen have
a new baby
called Bubble!

Almost all the mermaids thought the baby news was **great**.
But *Princess Meghan Sparkle* didn't **want** to celebrate.

She was baby Bubble's **sister**, but she found it all a **bore**.
From *Meghan's* point of view, her life was going **fine** before!

She could **play games** in the castle or **sing loudly** if she chose...

La - la - LAA!

138

...and always found a **quiet** place
to **read** or have a **doze**.

But now, the baby **screamed** so much,
it drove her up the wall,
and **smelled** so bad that *Meghan*
couldn't concentrate at all!

Wahhhh

One day, Meghan couldn't wait to read her book somewhere, when suddenly the sound of Bubble's **crying** filled the air.

So **Meghan** searched for somewhere **far away** from all the noise,

but every room was **smelly**...

full...

or **stuffed** with baby toys!

She slammed her book closed with a SMACK and shouted,
"IT'S NOT FAIR!

Everyone's gone baby mad: I can't read ANYWHERE."

Wahhhhhhhh!
wahhh!

She sped outside and swam along
a winding path at speed,
until she found a silent spot:
the **PERFECT** place to read!

Meghan read her book for **hours**,
as **happy** as a clam.

But **when** she tried to leave,
she cried ...

"I don't know where I am!"

Clownfish Corner

She'd swum out here too **quickly**,
and forgotten to keep track.
So now she simply **didn't know**
which path would take her back!

Just when she felt **all at sea**,
the princess heard a cough.
The **mail-turtle** was swimming by,
dropping parcels off.

Seaweed Stables

Whale Way

"**Your Royal Highness!**" Turtle cried,
and gave a little bow.

"Can you help me?" *Meghan* asked.
"I've **lost my way** somehow!"

"I'll take you home," said Turtle,
"but I **must** drop off this mail."
"That sounds fun!" the mermaid said,
and joined him on his trail.

First, he had a parcel for the **clownfish** family,
who all lived **cramped together** in a small anemone.

Thanks, Turtle!

"That looks **crowded**," Meghan thought,
and watched the clownfish play.
"I'm **lucky** I don't share a room
with Bubble every day."

Oooooooooh!

Ooooh!

A choir **singing** whale songs
was the next stop on their rounds.

But **Meghan** couldn't **understand**
the group's **unusual** sounds.

Turtle laughed:
"That's how they **speak**:
it just sounds odd to **you**."

Meghan thought of **Bubble's cries**...
could they mean something too?

They went to **Seaweed Stables** for their last delivery.
The little baby seahorses were racing with a

"wheeeeee!"

Meghan and the turtle
watched the babies for a while.

"Maybe siblings **are** ok,"
thought Meghan with a smile.

With the packages delivered,
Meghan thought of what she'd seen.
And **suddenly** she realised
how **silly** she had been!

She said, "I **understand** now
that when all is said and done,
having someone **new** around
is going to be **fun!**"

The turtle guided Meghan back across the ocean floor,
and soon she heard a distant cry she **knew** she'd heard before.

Wahhhhhhh!

"Thank you, Turtle!"
Meghan said.
"I recognise those sounds."
And then she followed Bubble's cries
into the castle grounds.

She rushed to **hug** the baby, feeling happy as can be.
"Hello Bubble," *Meghan* said. "I'm glad we're family."

After that, she didn't leave the royal baby's side, and read her **favourite** books aloud whenever Bubble cried.

So *Meghan* found some lovely friends, and as young Bubble grew,

she saw that life is wonderful when you are one of two!

Esme
the
Emerald
Fairy
and the Search for the Sparkle Stone

Sarah Creese * Lara Ede

In **Sparkle Town**, across a bridge,
almost hidden from sight,
there stood a small **museum**
with flags of green and white.

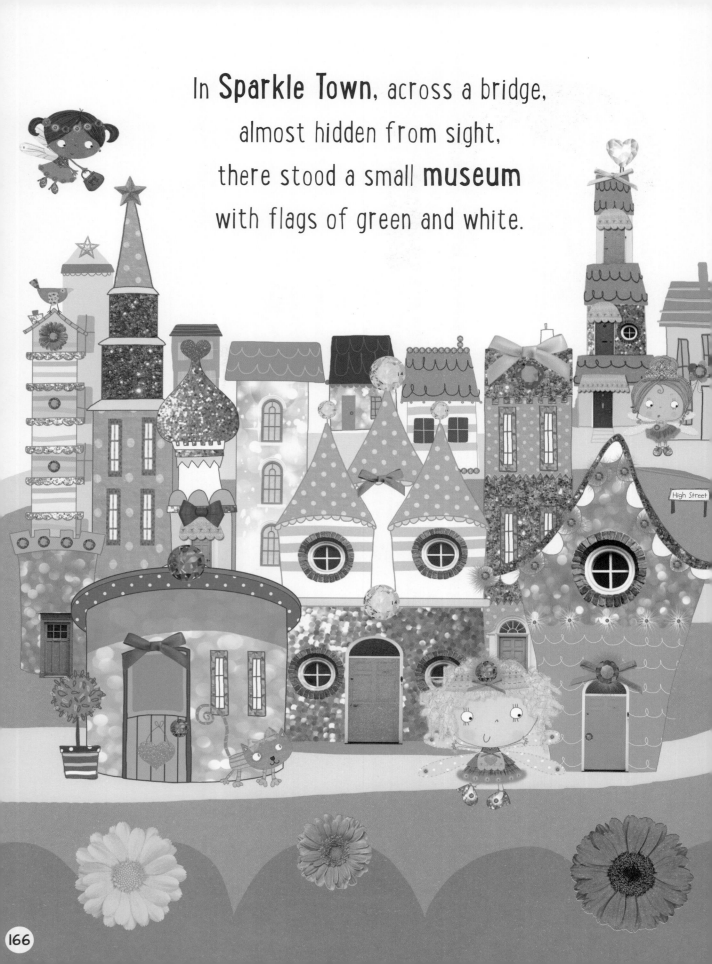

The museum kept all kinds of things,
from **books** to **giant bones**,
but best, and most amazing, were
its sparkling, precious **stones**.

Ooooooh!

Fairy-Rex

Esme the **Emerald Fairy**
looked after each display,
making sure her fairy guests
saw something **new** each day.

With one swish of her **emerald wand**,
she made each gem shine **bright**.

But because Esme was very **shy**,
she did this out of sight!

Esme **polished** every day,
but the fairies did not know,
for she did all this in **secret**,
too **shy** to let it show.

These are the sparkliest gems in town!

One morning, like each day before,
Esme began to work.
But when she waved her **wand**...

it FIZZED...

and POPPED...

then went **BERSERK!**

Without her wand, the sparkly stones became so **dull** and **plain** that the guests felt disappointed and they started to **complain!**

Oh, dear! These gems are sooo dull!

Well, I'm not coming here again.

173

Seeing their friend
look down and blue,
the fairies came to help.

But as they **cleaned**,
Susie **sneezed**, and knocked
a book from the shelf.

We can get
this place sparkling
in no time.

Achoo-oops!

THE MYSTERY OF THE SPARKLE STONE

The Sparkle Stone is the brightest gemstone in Fairy Land. It has not been seen for hundreds of years...

The Sparkle Stone will save the day!

Said Esme,
"Even with this book,
I'd **never** find the stone."

Daphne cried,
"We'll help you try —
you won't be on your own!"

As Esme felt uncertain still,
Susie took the lead.

And off they **flew** across the town
towards the **Silver Sea**.

At last they saw a mountaintop,
covered in shimmering white.
"The stone is near here," Esme said,
"that's why it's all **so bright!**"

With goggles on to shield their eyes
from all the dazzling snow,
the fairies **searched** from left to right,
then up and down below ...

They flew along a tunnel,
then saw, carved on a wall:

Ooh, what is this?

ONLY THOSE WITH INNER LIGHT MAY REACH THE SPARKLE HALL.

Each fairy gave the wall a tap,
but Esme felt too shy.
So the others, very gently,
encouraged her to try.

You can do it,
Esme!

Esme thought of her **museum**,
and what she had to save.
She took a breath, then tapped the wall,
"**Esme**," she said, "**BE BRAVE**."

The wall went **crrrRUNCH**,
then cracked apart.
Esme squeezed inside.
But in a **flash**,
it all turned black!
And she was **TERRIFIED!**

Before she had the time to think,
she felt her wand get **hot**.

It **SHOOK**
and **SHUDDERED**
and **SHIVERED**,
...then from her hand, it **shot!**
It whizzed into the darkness,
and into the unknown ...

...'til suddenly, the wand lit up **beneath** the **sparkle stone!**

The stone's bright light shone all around.
Esme stared **wide-eyed**:
a narrow path stretched towards the stone,
with big **DROPS** on each side.

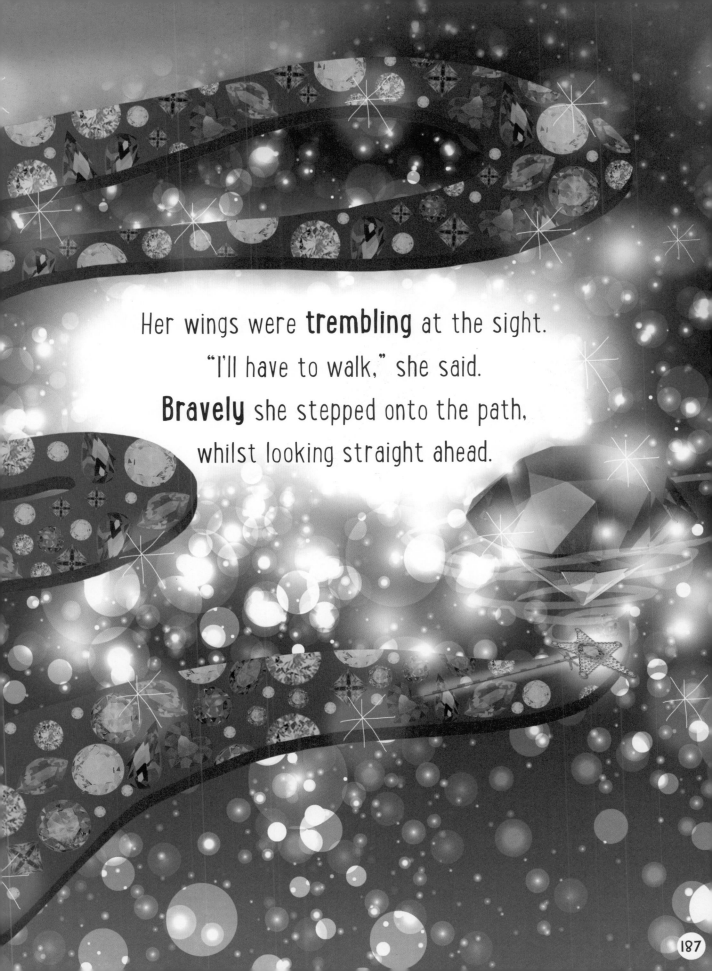

Her wings were **trembling** at the sight.
"I'll have to walk," she said.
Bravely she stepped onto the path,
whilst looking straight ahead.

With each new step, her **courage** grew,
and soon she reached the end.
She **boldly** took the stone and wand
and rushed back to her friends.

You did it, Esme!

Yippee!

Sleepily, but full of glee,
the fairies headed home.
And proudly, Esme put in place
the wondrous **SPARKLE STONE**.

Wow!

Soon, the museum was full again,
but **better** still than that,
was Esme's newfound **confidence**,
which brought her powers back!

What a super sight!

Now Esme's not afraid to show
just what **she can do**.

She **sparkles** on the outside —
and on the **inside**, too!